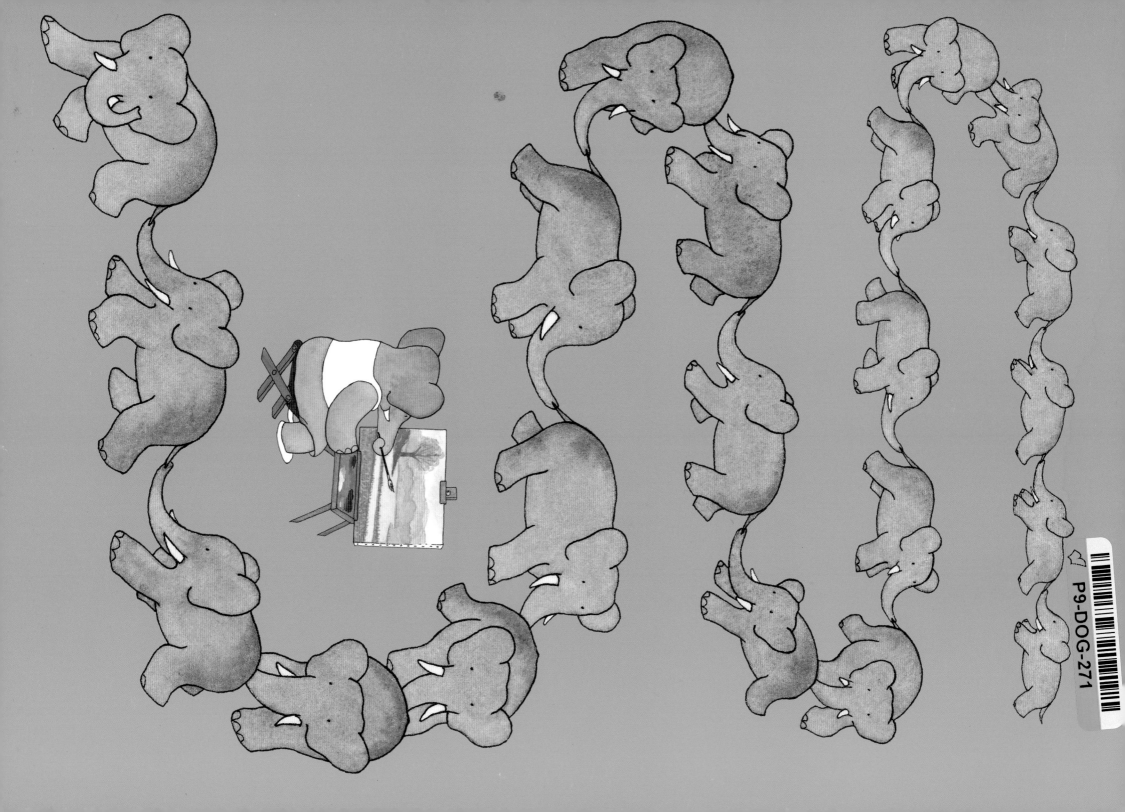

BABAR'S

MUSEUM OF ART

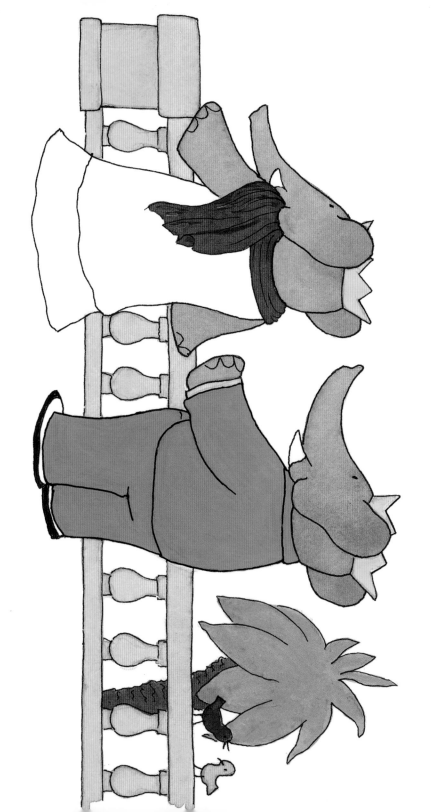

LAURENT DE BRUNHOFF

BABAR'S
MUSEUM OF ART
(Closed Mondays)

HARRY N. ABRAMS, INC., PUBLISHERS

Every Sunday, Babar and Celeste took their balloon up over Celesteville. One morning, they noticed the old railroad station standing empty on the far side of the lake.

"Elephants no longer take the train," said Babar. "They prefer to drive their cars. Look how the roads out of the city are jammed with traffic."

"What will happen to the train station?" asked Celeste. "It would be a shame to tear down such a beautiful building." She thought about the station as the balloon floated over the city.

"Here's an idea! All the art we've collected over the years needs a home. Why not make the station a museum?"

"Excellent thinking, Celeste!" said Babar.

9

They asked a famous architect to design the museum. She came to the palace to show the plans to Babar, Celeste, and their friend, old Cornelius. The work began without delay.

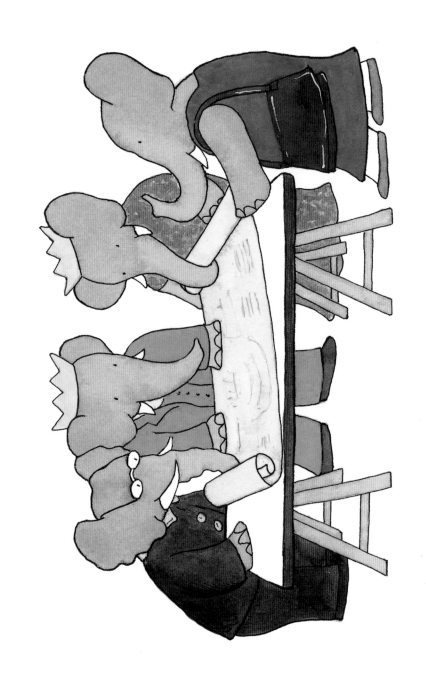

It took months to rebuild the station. Many elephants offered to help. Some did construction work.

11

Some carried the art from the palace basement, where Babar and Celeste stored what they had collected on their travels.

12

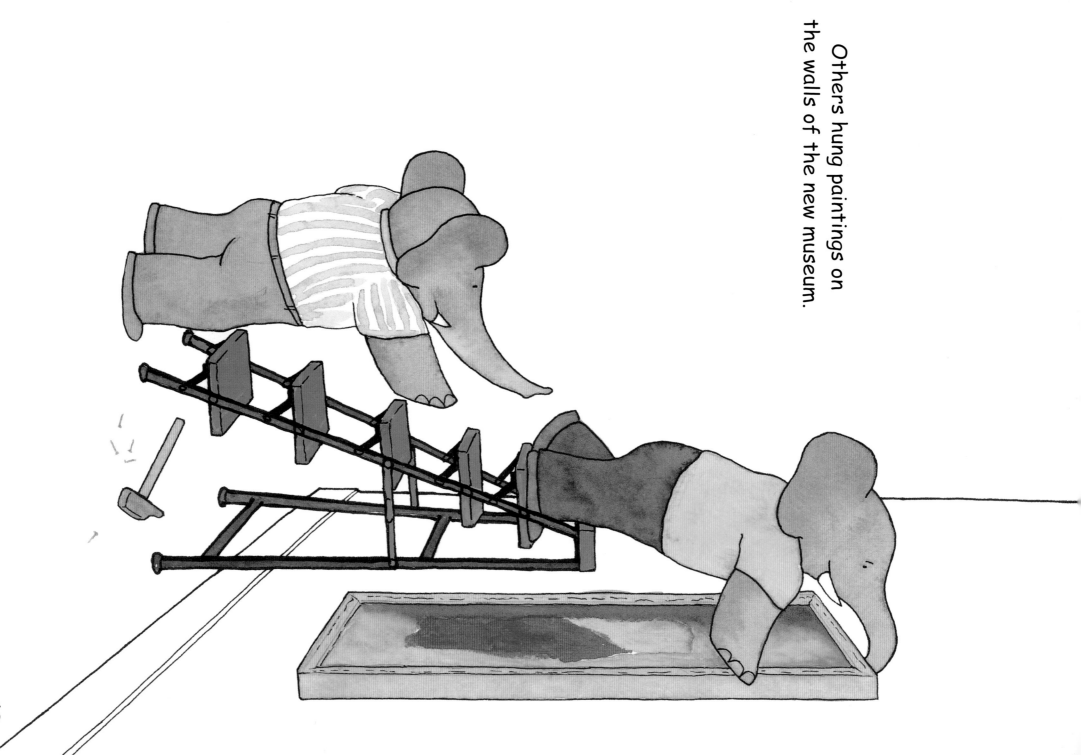

Others hung paintings on the walls of the new museum.

Finally, opening day arrived. Babar welcomed the citizens of Celesteville to their museum! An eager crowd followed Babar's family and close friends—Celeste, Flora, Pom, Alexander, Isabelle, cousin Arthur, his friend Zephir, the monkey, the Old Lady, and Cornelius—up the marble stairs, through the grand front doors, and into the building.

The children had never been to a museum before. "Will it be like school?" they wanted to know. "Will it be like church? Or like shopping or going on a picnic?"

"A little of all those things," said Celeste. "This museum is a building filled with works of art."

"But what are we supposed to do here?" Isabelle asked.

"How are we supposed to behave?"

"Look, don't touch, and tell me what you see," Celeste replied.

Flora stopped in front of a painting and said, "I see a little princess just like me, with her family and friends around her."

Isabelle chose a different picture. "I see another princess, and I would rather be this one. She has three cats, and she has the whole painting to herself."

Celeste smiled. "And you, boys?"

"I see a picnic," Alexander said, "and I wish we could have one."

"Yeah!" said Pom.

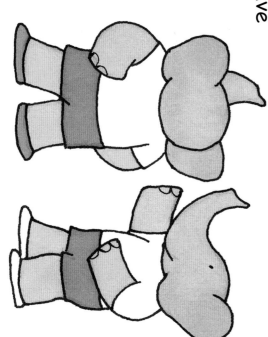

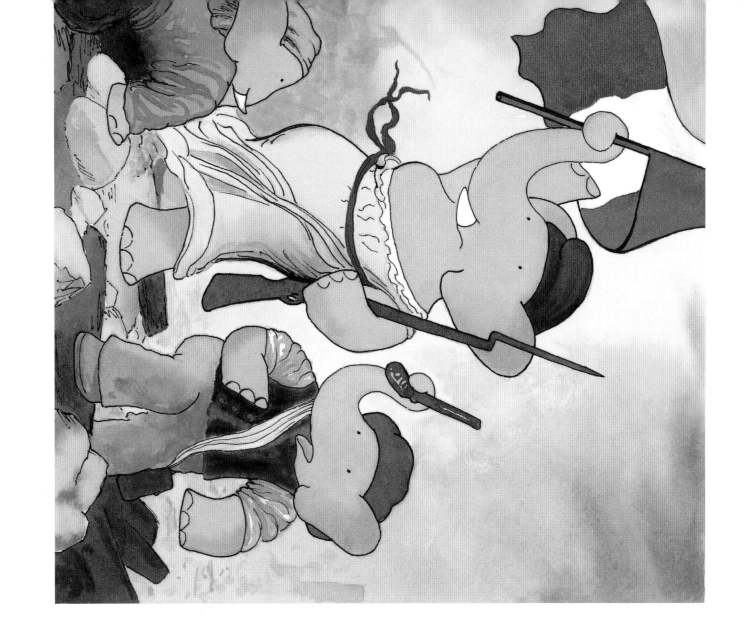

"I see a battle with soldiers, and I wish I was in it,"
said Arthur.
"Right! Me, too!" said Zephir.

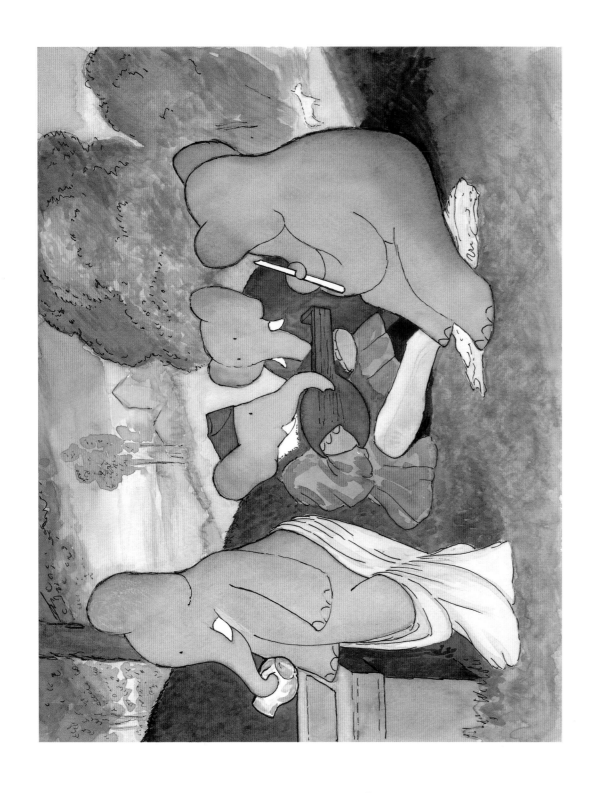

Dr. Capoulosse, the physician, said, "I like this one because they are making music."

"I like paintings that lift the mind and inspire great thoughts," Cornelius said. "This shows one wise elephant admiring another."

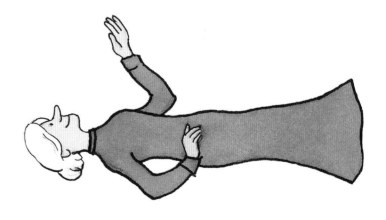

The Old Lady joined the discussion. "I like this," she said, "because it is peaceful. I feel calm when I look at it. The elephants do not get in each other's way."

25

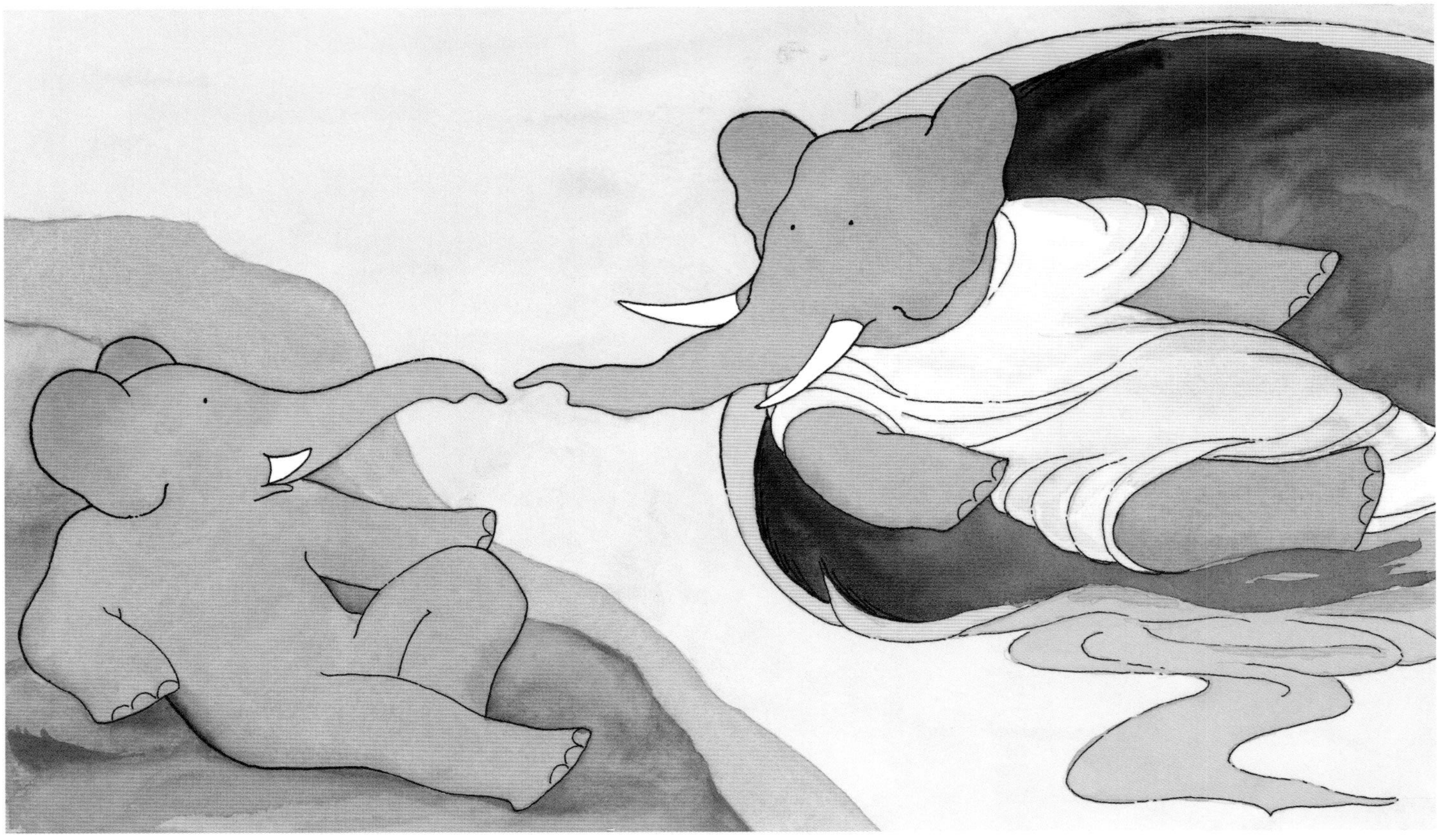

"Here we see the creation of the first elephant," said Cornelius. "That is a worthy subject. And excuse me, Isabelle, but the painting you thought showed a little girl is really of a little boy and the one that shows a battle, Arthur, is about winning freedom."

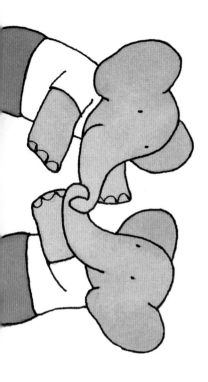

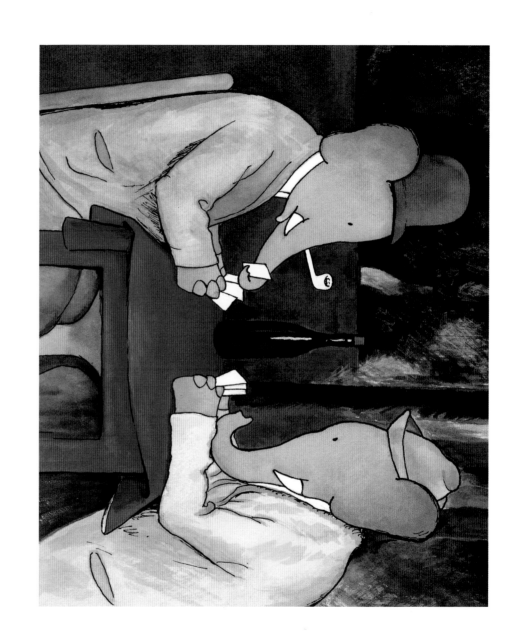

"Hush, Cornelius," said Celeste. "Let them have fun. They'll have plenty of lectures later."

But it did not matter because the children paid no attention to Cornelius.

"They're playing cards, and I like to play cards," said Alexander.

"Me, too," said Pom. "That's just what I was thinking."

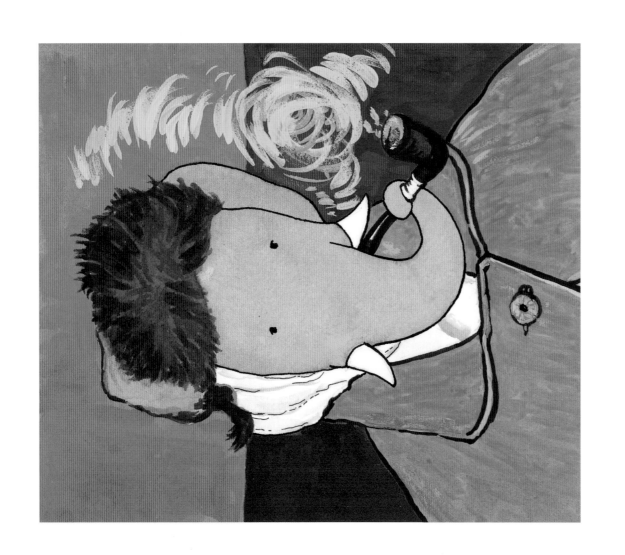

"I like this picture because it's red," said Arthur.

"I like the dog!" said Flora.

"The couple looks so happy together," said the Old Lady.

"I like the red," said Arthur, and Cornelius added, "The painter is trying to tell us something." But no one asked him to explain.

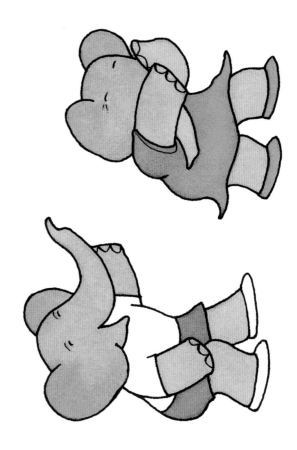

"This one," Alexander said laughing, "is telling us to dry off when we come out of the water."

"I see a woman who forgot to get dressed," said Arthur.

"It's about love," said Cornelius. "That 'woman' is Venus, the goddess of love."

"Hush, Cornelius," said Celeste.

"Does everything have to mean something in a picture?" Isabelle asked. "I like this picture of the jungle and my father on the sofa. I don't understand why the sofa's in the jungle, but I'm glad it is."

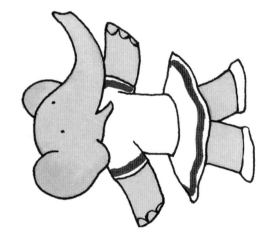

"Shouldn't it make sense?" Pom asked. "A fruit bowl can't be an elephant's leg."

"It's an elephant's head," said Isabelle. "See the ears and trunk?"

"I see what you mean, but that head is also a leg," Pom insisted. "Either way, it doesn't make sense."

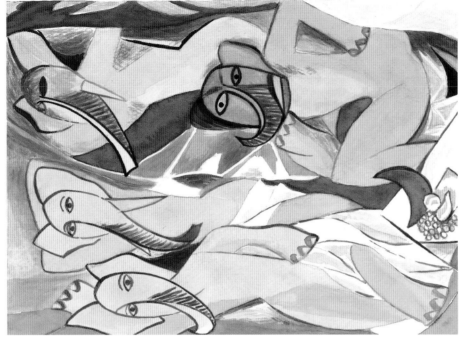

"Doesn't it have to be old to be in a museum?" asked Alexander.
"Doesn't it have to be pretty?" asked Flora.

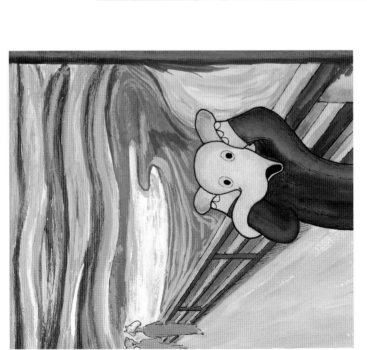

"It doesn't have to be or mean anything," said Babar. "There are no rules to tell us what art is."

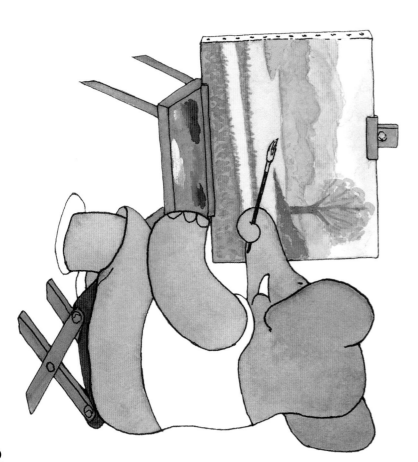

Soon the family moved on to the sculpture garden. Babar and Celeste had brought statues from all over the world to Celesteville.

36

"Will you take my dolls and put them in the museum?" Isabelle wondered.

"No, dear," said Celeste. "Don't worry."

37

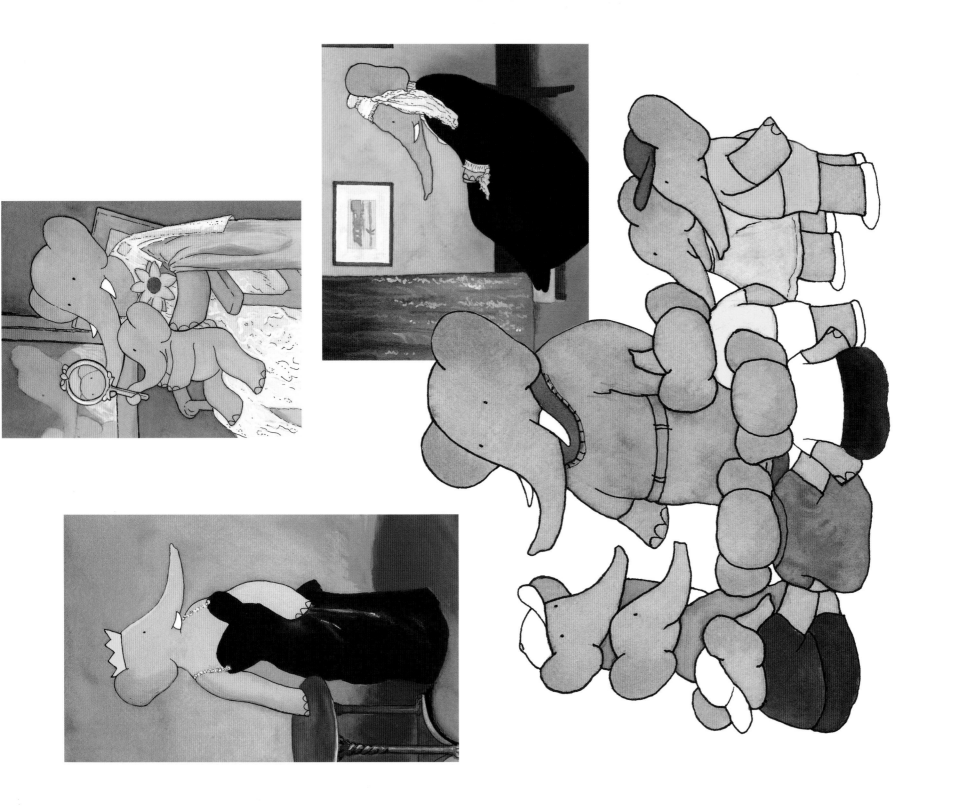

The elephants of Celesteville loved the new museum.

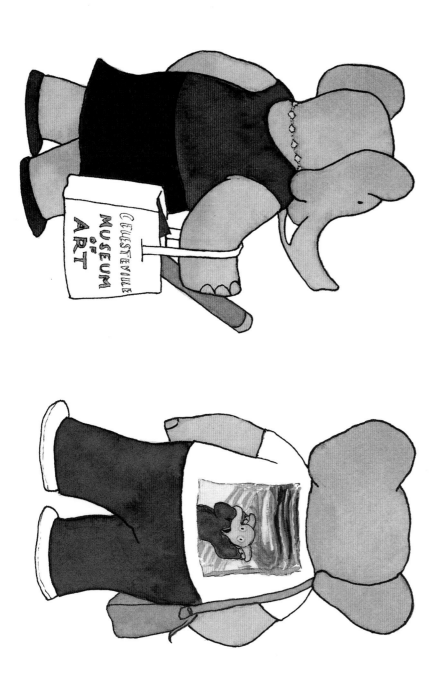

They went there to relax, to study, and to get ideas.

Babar and Celeste gave a party to celebrate the museum's success. The party was in the Egyptian wing, next to a temple that was rescued from a flood. Waiters passed refreshing lemonade.

40

Babar offered a toast. "I'd like to thank Celeste for suggesting we save the railroad station by making it into a museum. Three cheers for Celeste, and three cheers for art museums!"

41

Later Babar and Celeste took the children to meet the museum's artist-in-residence. They were able to watch him create a painting!

"I like that artist's work a lot," said Celeste when they left.

"So active. So lively."

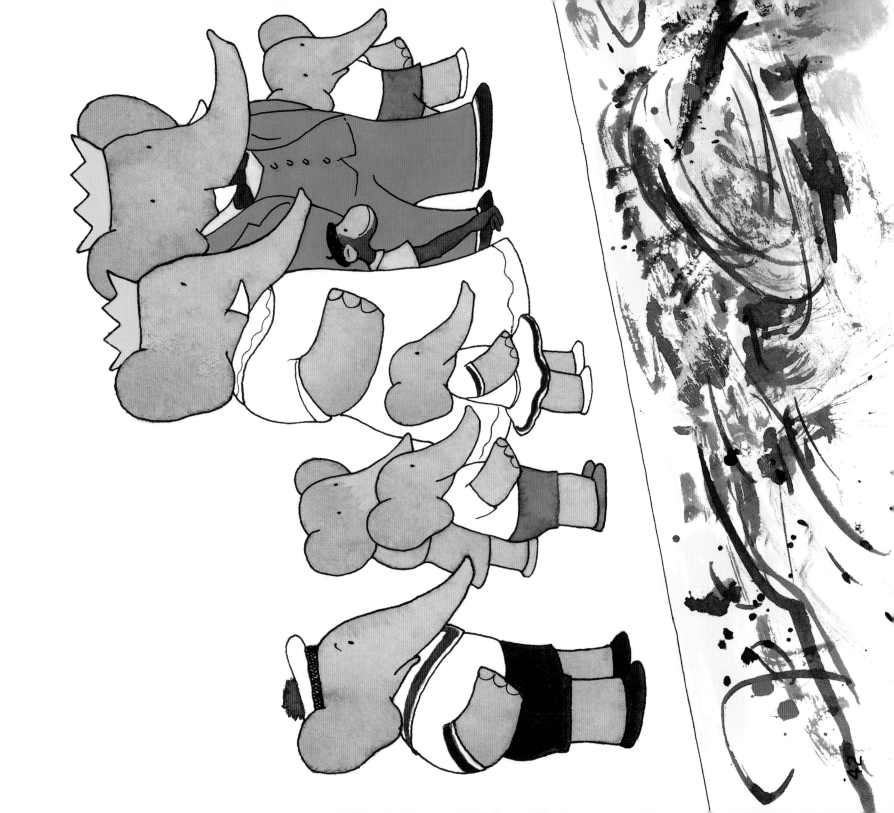

"Oh, I could do that myself," boasted Arthur. "I wish you would," said Babar. "I'm sure I will like what you do."

43

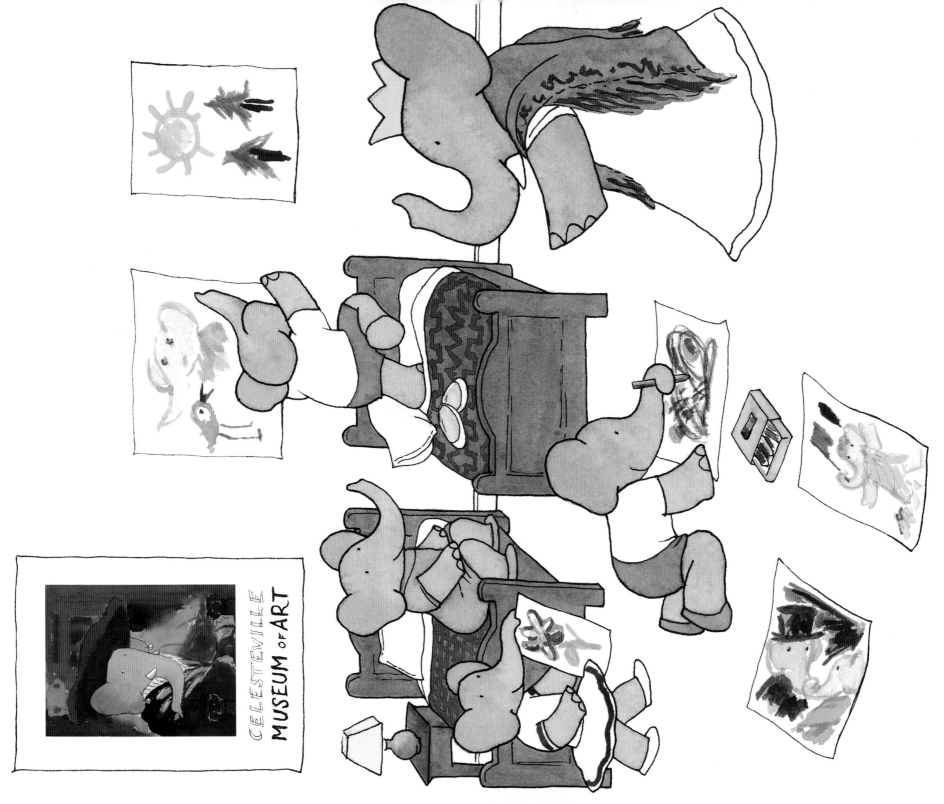

Back at home, the children drew pictures. They thought they might like to be artists when they grew up, or collect art, or teach, or make T-shirts. There were many possibilities, and they were all exciting.

CELESTEVILLE MUSEUM of ART

Babar and Celeste would like to thank all of the elephant and human friends who inspired their art collection and helped create the Celesteville Museum, especially:

Peter Paul Rubens (Rubens, His Wife Helena Fourment, and Their Son Peter Paul, page 14); Edouard Manet (The Balcony, page 14); Leonardo da Vinci (Mona Lisa, page 14); Raffaello Sanzio (Saint Michael and the Dragon, page 15); Anthony van Dyck (Charles I and Queen Henrietta Maria with Charles, Prince of Wales, and Princess Mary, page 15); Diego Velázquez (Las Meninas, page 17); Francisco de Goya (Don Manuel Osorio Manrique de Zuñiga, page 18); Pieter Brueghel the Elder (Harvest, page 19); Eugène Delacroix (Liberty Leading the People, pages 20-21); Tiziano Vecellio (Pastoral Concert, page 22); Rembrandt van Rijn (Aristotle with a Bust of Homer, page 23); Georges Seurat (A Sunday Afternoon on the Island of La Grande Jatte, pages 24-25); Michelangelo Buonarroti (The Creation of Adam, page 26); Paul Cézanne (The Card Players, page 27); Vincent van Gogh (Self-Portrait, page 28); Jan van Eyck (Portrait of Giovanni Arnolfini and His Wife Giovanna Cenami, page 29); Sandro Botticelli (Birth of Venus, pages 30-31); Henri Rousseau (The Dream, page 32); Salvador Dalí (Apparition of Face and Fruit Dish on a Beach, page 33); Edvard Munch (The Scream, page 34); Pablo Picasso (Les Demoiselles d'Avignon, page 34); René Magritte (The Human Condition, page 35); Anon., Hellenistic (Venus de Milo, page 36); Joel Shapiro (Untitled, page 36); Edgar Degas (little dancer, page 37); Aristide Maillol (female figure, pages 36-37); Anon., Hindu (Ganesh, page 37); Auguste Rodin (Balzac, page 37); John Singer Sargent (Madame Pierre Gautreau, page 38); Mary Cassatt (Mother and Child, page 38); J. A. M. Whistler (Arrangement in Black and Gray, page 38); Edouard Manet (Luncheon on the Grass, page 39); Anon., Nubian (Temple of Dendur, pages 40-41); Hans Namuth (Jackson Pollock at Work, pages 42-43); Jackson Pollock (One [Number 31, 1950], pages 42-43); Johannes Vermeer (Girl with a Red Hat, page 44); Gae Aulenti (architect of the Musée d'Orsay); Françoise Cachin (first director of the Musée d'Orsay); Howard Reeves, Linas Alsenas, and Becky Terhune of Harry N. Abrams, Inc.; and Clifford Ross, artist in many media.

Designer: Edward Miller

The artwork for each picture is prepared using watercolor on paper.
This text is set in 16-point Comic Sans.

Library of Congress Cataloging-in-Publication Data

Brunhoff, Laurent de, 1925-
Babar's museum of art / by Laurent de Brunhoff.
p. cm.
Summary: Babar and Celeste convert Celesteville's old railroad station into an art museum containing famous masterworks featuring elephants.
ISBN 0-8109-4597-5
[1. Art museums—Fiction. 2. Museums—Fiction. 3. Elephants—Fiction. 4. Animals in art—Fiction.] I. Title.

PZ7.B82843 Bab† 2003
[E]—dc21

2002156489

Harry N. Abrams, Inc.
100 Fifth Avenue
New York, N.Y. 10011
www.abramsbooks.com

Abrams is a subsidiary of
LA MARTINIÈRE
GROUPE

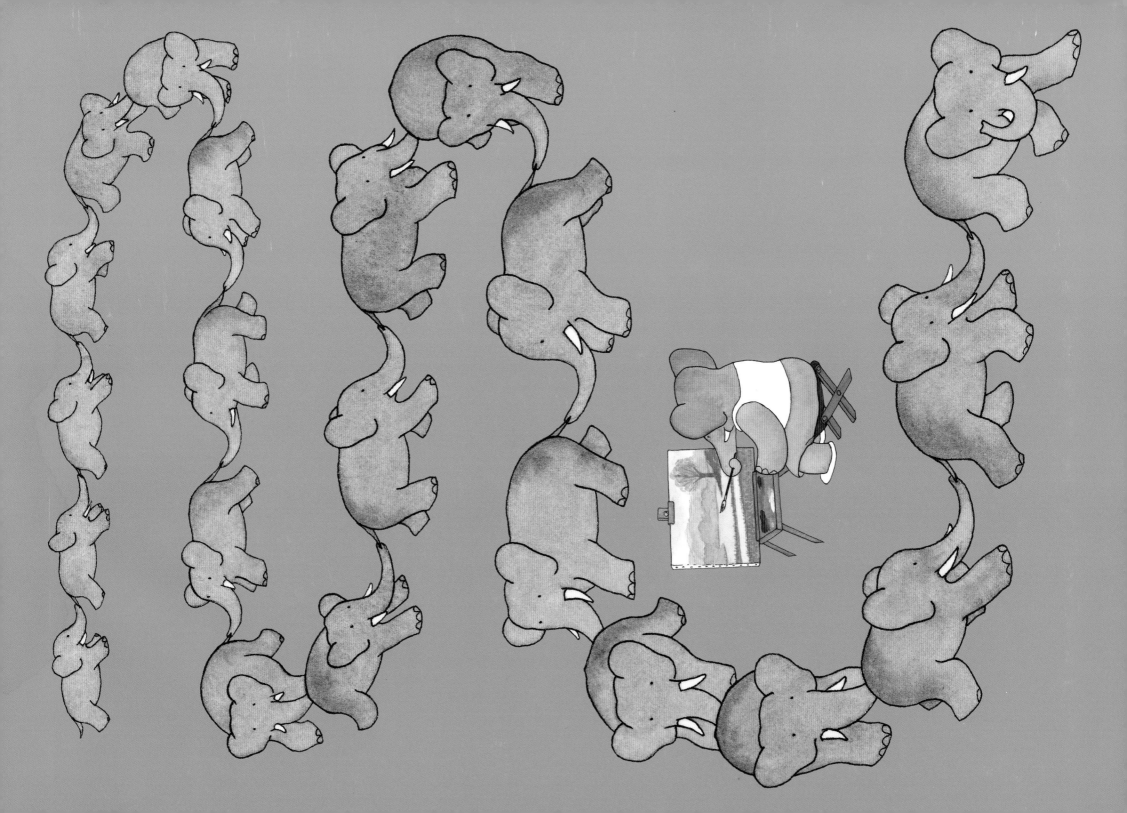